Stories Heard Around The Lunchroom

James Flanagan

authorHOUSE®

AuthorHouse™
1663 Liberty Drive
Bloomington, IN 47403
www.authorhouse.com
Phone: 1-800-839-8640

First published by AuthorHouse 2/22/2010

ISBN: 978-1-4490-8443-1 (sc)

Printed in the United States of America
Bloomington, Indiana

This book is printed on acid-free paper.

Dedicated to Eileen, Cat, Jared, Megan and over 20,000 students whom I've known and cared for

I would like to thank my editor Lyn Chamberlain, Megan Flanagan, Dale Herron and the many wonderful storytellers who have helped me in the past 7 years. I especially want to thank Lyn Ford who got me started in storytelling.

Table of Contents

Around The Lunchroom

Outwardly, the lunchroom looks normal, but it's actually full of weird and interesting happenings. These happenings become stories. Stories are what this book is all about—stories about kids just dealing with life.

Let's start right here in the lunchroom.

Some cafeteria food is very colorful. I've seen purple fuzz on my pizza, green ham, and scrambled eggs that change color in different light. Of course, there is mystery meat, unheard of vegetables, and the pudding. Pudding you cannot tell is pudding. The kids say some food looks better thrown up than eaten. They may be right. After enough samples of school cafeteria food, your stomach becomes biologically resistive to all forms of disease.

In the lunchroom, there is always a division between those who bought and those who did not. The "brought" people have containers that range from a basic brown bag to ice coolers that freeze everything solid in five minutes flat. We tried it once

1

with an English book. Sure enough, it froze the volume in no time.

Last year, there was a kid who carried his lunch in a pizza delivery box. Everything he had for lunch must fit into this box. You could give him anything; he could fold it to fit that box. The worst experience was the time he packed a large piece of chocolate cheesecake. By lunchtime, his cake resembled roadkill on a hot pavement.

I sometimes feel bad for some of the brownbaggers. Every week, you see a bagger grasping a lunch bag by the very top and holding it over the trash container. Something leaked. The bottom of the bag is full of what can only be called muddy soup. No matter what they say on TV, plastic bags do leak liquid.

Some kids make lunch an art form. They bring veggies, granola biscuits, dip, colorful napkins and a juice with a name you can't pronounce.

I always like to wait until about the fourth veggie has been dipped before pointing to something moving in the dip. Of course, if you time this just right, the dipper's crisis causes milk to issue from students' noses. Milk exiting another person's nose is always a scream.

Each week, some kid gets peanut butter stuck on the roof of their mouth. Usually, everybody understands and just nods to the kid. It sounds like he is speaking a strange nasal language. He or she— usually it's a boy—roams around until he can scoop the peanut stuff out of his mouth.

There is always someone somewhere in the lunchroom who had a bologna sandwich and simply does not get it. However, someone else will say, "Here bite into this," and give the kid a piece of their peanut butter and jelly sandwich. A minute later that child talks funny and indicates that he now understands the problem.

After years of experience, the cafeteria staff learned to keep special spoons on hand for such emergencies.

Flies and bees invade the cafeteria during the warm days. Many an insect has been eaten as part of a lunch. Girls seem to do this more than boys. Boys actually love this lunchtime happening—especially when it happens to someone else. I have witnessed a digested bug produce screaming fits in a girl who would head for the bathroom as fast as she could go.

Occasionally, mashed potatoes or pudding finds its way onto seats. Guys pull this prank on other guys. Doing this to a girl means certain death. Once in awhile, a girl pulls this on a boy, an event that calls for much gutting it out. *Never let a girl know she's gotten the better of you* is the boys' motto.

Teachers patrol the lunchroom. Most are rather easy on enforcing the rules. Chocolate chip bribery is rampant among lunchroom supervisors. Food fights and juice squirts happen with some regularity.

I have seen food flying very close to a teacher's body. Only a miracle prevents contact. Teachers catch a glimpse of something going past. However they don't recognize the blur as food. Kids will be wet for no apparent reason. Quiet in the lunchroom usually means a target has received a direct hit. Quiet alerts the supervising adult. As quickly as the fight starts, it's over. Ooos are saved until later. Food launches are often replayed in class after lunch.

Flirting is refined in the lunchroom. You look when she's not looking. When she turns toward you, you look away. What guys never realize is that girls watch out for other girls. The object of your attention will be informed by her best friend that you are gazing upon her.

Occasionally, if you watch, you can catch other stories in the lunchroom. Kids seem to let down their guard at lunch. And still, many important stories go completely unnoticed.

Look at that table by the wall. See the kid sitting all by himself at one end of the table. He pays no attention to the girls sitting there. They are discussing what they are going to do tonight, what movie they might see and who will be at the show. He keeps his head down and says nothing.

He can't think about going out tonight or any other evening. Last night about midnight, his little brother ran into his room and hid in his bed. Their mom and dad were fighting again. He has always protected his little brother on nights like this. He holds his brother until the little body relaxes. He stays awake while his brother sleeps, so he comes to school tired. Some know about his family, but no one talks about it. There are quite a few of these unknown heroes in schools. You can catch them in the lunchroom if you look carefully.

That's Jason over by the window. He's a really good guy and the best runner in school. He barely gets by on the reading, though. I think the teachers give him a break.

When we got to reading class the first day of school this year, we all picked up our books. Mrs. Cranston asked each of us to read. The bell rang just before Jason's turn. We all felt very bad for him the next day. We knew what would happen. He would stutter over the words and then sit down before the teacher asked him to.

Well, Mrs. Cranston came in, took attendance, and asked, "Where did we stop?"

The whole class just looked down at our books, hoping she forgot and skipped over Jason's name. That didn't happen.

Jason stood up with his reading book in his hands. I couldn't look at his face. Jason started to read— slowly at first, but then he picked up speed and before we knew it, he finished an entire paragraph. Jason started to read the second paragraph and the teacher stopped him. She thanked him. We all sat up in amazement. I looked at Jason. He had a big smile on his face. I looked up at Mrs. Cranston. She had a big smile on her face, but there were tears in her eyes.

You know something. I had tears in my eyes, too. It was the best reading class we had in a long time.

You have to keep your eyes open in this school. Lots of things happen. The big news was that the prankers of the fifth grade got caught, but that's another story later in this book.

See Randy, over there eating pizza. Randy has a story heard just last week in the lunchroom.

The Word That Backfired

Randy was the class clown. He liked a particular word. He used it to make boys laugh and girls cringe. The word is "booger."

Randy wrote it in notes, whispered it in ears and invented unique ways to make people laugh. For example, Randy especially liked the new movie title, Harry Potter and the Chamber of Boogers. This written on a piece of paper traveled around the fifth grade one afternoon causing quite a commotion.

Mrs. Beck revised her seating chart after this incident. Randy was seated behind Emily. He began to terrorize Emily by whispering "Booger" to her at least once an hour.

The second day, Emily warned Randy to stop. This did not even faze Randy.

The following day was Thursday. At 9:01 a.m. Emily told Randy to stop. At 9:03 a.m. Randy said the Word and whack! Emily hit Randy.

Mrs. Beck hauled Emily out into the hall. While the teacher understood Emily's complaint, she could not accept hitting especially in the classroom. Emily received a detention.

Emily marched back into the room. If looks could kill, the entire right side of the room would be gone. Randy did not look at Emily, but you could see his smile under his bowed head.

Emily vowed revenge. For the next week, Emily tried really hard to listen every time Randy said "booger." She even practiced it at home!

About two weeks later the class was working on a writing assignment when someone said something. "Booger."

It sounded like yes, booger.

"Who said that?" asked Mrs. Beck.

No one answered but every student looked at Randy.

Randy looked back with an "I didn't say it" expression on his face.

The word came again.

Mrs. Beck stood up from her desk. She scanned the class.

"Booger."

"Randy, is that you?" asked Mrs. Beck.

"No," answered Randy.

"Randy, that is your so-called favorite word!" explained the teacher.

"Booger."

"Stop that!" Mrs. Beck called to Randy.

The class started to giggle and look directly at Randy. Emily sat in her seat quietly. She turned and looked directly at Randy.

"Booger."

"Randy out in the hall," ordered the teacher.

Randy was freaked. He argued that it was not him.

"But it sounds just like you," said Mrs. Beck. Randy received his detention.

Not believing that this had happened, Randy returned to his seat. He just sat there.

The day ended and the students filled out to their buses. Randy found his seat. He still couldn't believe what had happened.

A girl sitting behind Randy tapped him on the shoulder and pointed toward the bus beside them. Emily was waving at Randy. She held up a book to the window. The title was Ventriloquism Made Easy.

Emily and the kids around Randy laughed. Randy did not crack a smile.

No one messed with Emily. That class' English was "boogerless" the rest of the year.

The Principal and the Bullinators

After twelve weeks, the campaign against bullies produced results. However one particularly clever boy still plyed his bullying art. Mr. Franklin, the principal, was always on the lookout, but he was never able to pin anything specific on the boy. Joshua remained a nasty bully who picked on kids and scared them into keeping quiet.

Right after Joshua bullied Adam's sixth-grade cousin, Adam called a meeting of three students to deal with the "J" situation. Adam, Joey, and Shawn organized the Bullinators. These three young men were very similar in looks and actions. They measured about five feet, five inches. They were blond. They were smart, although their school grades didn't show it. And, I must add, they had all spent time in the principal's office.

The last incident involved turning a seventh-grade girl into a human fire siren. The three had conspired to put a live mouse in her locker. The mouse went into the locker alive, but after a few smacks with a purse, the little guy left dead. Of course, the body disappeared, but well, that's another story.

The Bullinators started its campaign of retaliation. Two weeks ago, Joshua lost his socks after gym class. Two days later, his pants came up missing. For some reason, this made him unusually angry.

"No one messes with me!" he told several people.

Joshua always enjoyed looking at himself in the mirror hanging on the inside of his locker. One week after the missing pants incident, he opened his locker to find a note attached to his mirror. "Object in mirror is dumber than appears," he read.

Joshua was really getting angry. He knew someone was up to these pranks, but no one knew who. He asked or strong-armed almost everyone in his grade.

It was time for the master stroke, and Mr. Franklin caught it in the planning stages. One day as he made his end-of-the-day rounds, he spied a strange drill. The three blond bullinators were crowded around a locker. Two hurried to do some activity and then jumped back. The third timed them with a stopwatch.

As they completed another drill, Mr. Franklin walked up.

"What are you guys doing?" he asked.

All the boys jumped about a foot high and immediately started making excuses.

"Whose locker is this?" demanded the principal.

"Mine," answered Adam.

"Open it, I want to inspect it for mice."

After inspecting the locker, Mr. Franklin grilled the three on what they were doing.

They remained quiet.

"Adam, report to my office first period tomorrow," he ordered.

"Why me?" asked Adam.

The principal gave him a look and Adam agreed to come without further complaint.

The next morning, Adam arrived at the principal's office. He was a bit nervous.

"Adam, what's up?" the principal asked.

"Nothing, Mr. F."

"Okay Adam, you can stand there until I get some answers. Of course, you are going to get very tired and hungry and oh yes, there is the bathroom issue," smiled Mr. F.

"Listen, Mr. F, I can't tell you what we're doing. But I think you'll like it," Adam said.

"Is anyone going to get hurt?"

"No!" answered Adam.

"Mr. F, if you'll be in the back hall just about two minutes before the end of second period tomorrow, you'll see it all. And I guarantee no one will get hurt. It that a deal?"

The principal agreed and Adam left for class.

The next day Mr. Franklin set the timer. Three minutes before the end of second period, the principal headed for the back hall. As he approached the corner, three small blond racers passed him flying low. Being an experienced principal, he moved forward cautiously and peeked around the corner.

Joshua, the bully, had his back to his locker. He seemed to be held there against his will. The more he struggled, the worst it became. After watching for a minute, Mr. Franklin realized he had to do something. He went into action. He turned around and walked back to his office with a girm look on his face. The bell ending the period rang just as he started toward his office.

"Nuts," he said under his breath.

He turned around and walked toward the stuck bully. As he approached, he heard laughter. The closer he came to the bully, the louder the laughter.

Joshua was almost in tears. No one had ever laughed at him. Mr. Franklin worked to release the bully by doing the combination lock. The locker door opened and released the belt holding Joshua.

The halls cleared and the next bell rang. Mr. Franklin escorted Joshua to his next class. As they entered the classroom, a hush fell over the students. The principal explained the situation quietly to the teacher and left.

About the time he closed the door, the laughter started.

Returning to the office, the principal found that the incident was known all over the school. He was about to call the three commandos to the office, when Joshua appeared in the doorway.

"I'm sick."

"OK," the principal said the secretary, "take his temperature, please."

Joshua had no temperature and was sent back to class. Twenty minutes later, he was back, feeling worse. Mr. Franklin decided to let the secretary call his mother.

Within minutes Mom was in the office to sign Joshua out of school.

As the mother left the office, the principal began to count to 10. At 8 she re-entered the office. She was very angry.

"My poor Joshua is a nervous wreak. How could you let this happen?" she cried.

Before the principal could answer, the mother informed him she was going to take this to the superintendent.

With hate in her eyes, the mother left the office slamming the door behind her.

The principal called on the intercom for the three boys to come to the office. Over the intercom, he could hear cheering as the three left the classroom.

They arrived looking like heroes.

The principal was about to speak when the secretary entered the office.

"Superintendent Richardson is on the phone," she said, looking worried.

The principal pointed to the boys to wait outside.

The superintendent explained that Joshua's mother had just left his office. "She was hopping mad and she wants the evil doers punished."

Mr. Franklin thoughtfully agreed.

The three boys were recalled to the principal's office.

"You will all have to received discipline for your actions today," he told the boys.

"Aw, Mr. F, he deserved it and you know it," said Adam.

"That may be true, but if it was done to you, I would react the same way."

"OK," said Joey, "but we wouldn't need such a thing to happen to us."

"I will call all your parents. Now go back to class—and of course, your cheers," Mr. Franklin said as he waved them out of his office.

The "cheers" comment brought smiles to all three boys' faces. In fact, as they left the office and passed the study hall, the students applauded.

The secretary voiced her disapproval. "How can they be disciplined. That jerk deserved it!"

Mr. Franklin ignored her comment and started making his phone calls.

All the parents understood that rules must be upheld. Before she hung up, Shawn's mother commented, "I know you have to do this, but for me, I am going to give my son a big hug."

The boys were to report to Room 112 on Friday at 2:35 p.m. promptly.

Friday arrived. The boys were heroes. The bully maintained a very low profile. He need not try to get even. The three bullinators had arranged for several of the larger football players to provide escort to and from classes. The three boys had planned for everything except the detention they were about to serve.

The principal told the boys to go to the Room 112, while he talked to their bus driver.

Mr. Franklin returned to make sure the boys signed in. At 2:41, he announced that the detention was over. "Your bus is waiting. So hurry on out to it."

The boys got on the bus and it started its crawl down the school driveway. As it turned onto the highway, Mr. Franklin heard a great cheer. Justice had been served.

You're in Big Trouble Now

Laura and Marty were brother and sister. AND they did not get along well. They picked on each other. They fought and they were driving their parents crazy with their behavior.

About 2 months ago, Laura came home from school and went up to her room. She had two china dolls that had been her aunts. Laura kept them on her pillows. As she walked into the room, there were the dolls on the pillow as usual—without their heads. Laura screamed and ran down to show the headless dolls to Mom.

Mom turned to Marty. Marty had this blank I-didn't-do anything look on his face. Mom was not fooled. "You're in big trouble now!" she said.

Marty went to bed right after dinner. He was going to do this until the heads returned. The trouble was that Marty forgot where he hid the heads. Laura did not believe him for a second.

Two days later the heads had still not been returned to the china dolls. So Laura accidentally put Marty's favorite ball cap in the dishwasher and turned it on. The ball cap came out looking very little like the favorite Marty held so dear.

Mom looked at the washed out cap and informed Laura, "You're in big trouble now!'

Laura was going to bed right after dinner until she came up with the money to pay for a new cap.

At least things were quiet after dinner.

But that was to change.

Marty was cleaning out the garage as part of his not hiding the doll heads when he found some old, empty Girl Scout Cookie boxes. They gave him a great idea. He put the boxes in a big plastic bag and hid them under his bed. No one in their right mind would ever go putting their hand under his bed.

Marty waited.

Ten days later, Laura, a Girl Scout, brought home a new batch of cookies to take to school. She had sold all 12 boxes to the teachers. As a precaution, Mom suggested they put them out on the back porch to keep them cool until they could be taken to school.

After everyone had gone to sleep, Marty snuck down to the porch. He put the new boxes in the kitchen pantry and scattered the old boxes around the back porch. Giggling he returned to bed.

Marty was the first one down to breakfast. He could not wait to see Laura's face. And he did. Laura yelled for Mom and then started to cry.

Mom found Laura in the middle of the mess. She tried to calm Laura and went to the pantry. There she found the new cookies. She glared at Marty, who was trying to hide under the kitchen table. "You're in big trouble!" she said in a loud voice.

Guess who went to school with Mom and guess who waited in the rain for the bus.

Now there are some groups you should not mess with, the Marines, the FBI and the Girl Scouts. Marty could not believe how much trouble he was in.

When school ended, he ran to the bus and sat right behind the driver for safety. Every Girl Scout to get on the bus glared at him, mouthing threats under their breath.

The bus stopped at Marty and Laura's house. Marty ran to the back porch, Laura in chase. He got to the porch door; he opened it and stopped dead in his tracks. Laura grabbed him and lifted her fist, but then she stopped, too. They both stood there looking at what was on that porch—the prettiest collie puppy they had ever seen.

Mom opened the door and they jumped up to hug her and thanked her. They had always wanted a puppy.

"This is great! What are we going to name the puppy?" Laura asked.

"The question is, are you going to keep him?" answered Mom.

"What?" they said at once.

Mom explained that their behavior had to stop. She felt the puppy would be the answer. To keep the dog, they would have to take care of the puppy together *And* stop fighting with each other.

To underscore this way to keep the dog, Mom said they would not be able to name the dog for a month. That month was plenty of time for them to learn to work together and behave.

The dog worked a miracle. The doll heads were found and returned. Marty got a new ball cap. The kids took turns caring for the puppy.

With only two days to go until the dog was really theirs, Laura and Marty began to think of names for their beloved puppy.

They were discussing that very issue when they opened the back porch door to discover the dog was gone. His bowl was there and just a piece of rope used to tie the puppy.

They had to find that dog before Mom found out. If she found they had not taken proper care of the puppy, it would surely go back.

They searched all over the neighborhood. Laura went as far as the freeway, but there was no trace of the dog.

They arrived back to the porch steps to sit and cry. Just at the moment, Laura got a great idea.

"The puppy always comes when you yell. So you just holler as loud as you can," she said to Marty.

Marty yelled, but it just did not seem loud enough.

"Take off your shoe," ordered Laura.

"What?" Marty asked.

"Just do it."

Marty did and Laura had him stick his foot out. "When I count to three you yell. Okay?" explained the sister.

On three, as Marty started to yell, Laura stamped down on his foot. That "puppy" was probably heard in the next town.

While Marty was hopping around holding his toe, they both listened. No dog was coming.

"Okay, let's try your other toe!" said Laura.

"Oh no you don't. It's your turn," answered Marty.

Laura took off her shoe but warned Marty not to stamp real hard.

On three, Marty stepped on Laura's toe as she yelled, "Puppy!"

No dog sounds were heard.

Both kids sat down on the steps to nurse their toes when around the corner of the garage came their dog. It was dirty and had leaves and twigs stuck in its hair. They didn't care. They just hugged that dog.

Suddenly, the door opened and Mom came out on the porch.

She asked," Why is the dog so dirty?"

The kids explained that the puppy got loose. "We stepped on each other's toes and we got the puppy back." said Laura.

Mom was not sure about the toe thing but she was happy about the outcome. She decided to let the time period end right now.

The kids were so happy they didn't know whom to hug first. But Mom decided she would name the dog. Laura's and Marty's puppy's name is "You're in Big Trouble." They call him Trouble for short.

DOVWAL

Ralph is black with white spots and a white nose. She has long hair and ears that blow in the wind when she rides in the back seat of the car and sticks her head out the window. She's a good-natured, gentle dog, but real smart, smarter than my sister. Yeh, Ralph is a she. Mom and my sister named her Raphaelle, but I couldn't bring myself to call her that. Especially in front of my friends. So I call her Ralph.

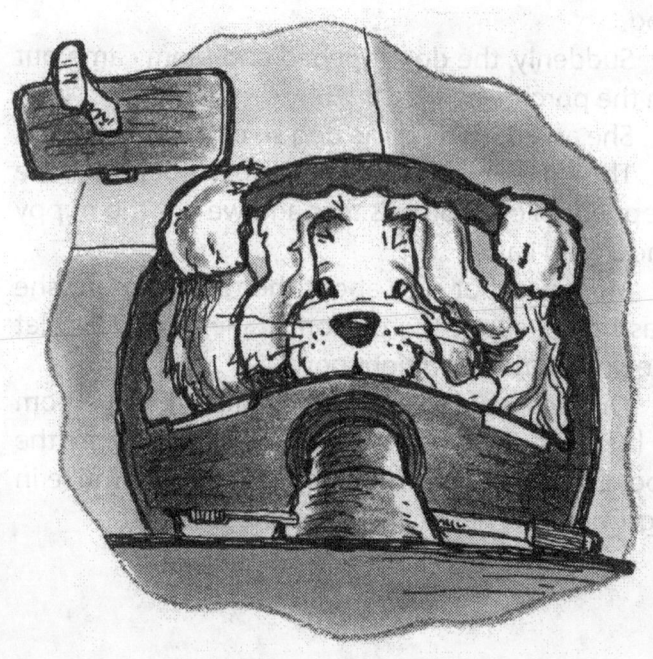

The car that Ralph likes best is a yellow and brown (the brown is rust) 1969 Dodge something. Very little works on it. The gas gauge is broken, and at night, if you want to honk the horn, you have to turn off the lights.

As I said, the gas gauge is broken, so we never know if we have any gas. I put a gas can in the trunk just in case.

That's where the whole mess started.

My sister—her name is Melody. Melody, cheez! They should have called her Sour Notes. Anyway, she's 16 and drives. Not real well. So Dad only lets her use the 1969 Dodge something.

Well, this one Thursday morning, Mom sent us to the store for groceries. Ralph went along. Mom didn't care, because the inside of the car was so bad Ralph couldn't mess up anything.

We were driving down Hill Street when the car puttered to a stop. No gas.

Of course, Ol' Mel started chewing. "Look," I said, "we can get some gas at George's Gas Station." The station was only about half a block away.

We left Ralph in the 1969 yellow something. We had no sooner started toward the station, though, when we heard Ralph bark. I turned around and watched her jump into the front seat. Her paws must have hit the gear shift bar, because the car started moving.

There is Ralph, her head hanging out the window and the breeze blowing her ears. Ralph's front paws were on the wheel. She really looked like she knew what she was doing.

"Oh my gosh, we got to get her," Ol' Mel said. Well, duh!

Just then, George, the gas station owner, looks out and says, "Why, there's no one driving that car."

I yelled back, "Yes there is, Ralph's driving it!"

"Ralph?" George hollered, and took off chasing Ralph along with us. I suppose he intended for Bob, his assistant, to stay and pump gas, but Bob started running, too.

I saw Jim Ford's bike in his yard and I jumped on it.

I caught up with Ralph pretty quick. I yelled to get her attention.

She turned to look at me. But she still had her paws on the steering wheel and the car pulled toward me.

The next thing I know I'm upside down in the Macks' yard.

Ralph is looking at me, then back at the road. Both paws are on the steering wheel and she doesn't have a care in the world.

George caught up with the car and grabbed the back fender.

You should have seen the look on his face when that fender came off in his hands. He just sat there in the middle of the street holding a rusty car fender.

Ol' Melody, Bob, and me just passed him right by.

"Ralph's headed across Main! Then Hill Street goes up. That'll stop her," Bob yelled.

Just at that very moment, Nasty, the Dood's cat, came out of the alley right before Main. Ralph saw him, turned and barked—with her paws on the steering wheel, of course.

That caused the car to turn on to Main just as pretty as you please.

As Ralph turned, he passed Sheriff Johnson who took one look at the yellow something with a dog driving. He screamed something and made a U turn right in the middle of Main Street. He jumped out of his car and took off in hot pursuit.

It was early and no one was out. The street was clear. Well, except for Mrs. Bodice. She was walking across the street in the crosswalk by the grocery store. When she saw Ralph coming, she made a you-better-stop-it face and held up her cane.

She looked hard at the yellow something, recognized Ralph, and fainted dead away. Bob stopped to help her and I ran to catch the car.

It finally slowed down naturally. I opened the driver's side door and jumped in. Ralph was just licking happy to see me.

But I didn't know how to drive as well as Ralph.

Ol' Melody hollered, "Step on the brake!"

Oh, yeh, right. I looked down and saw three pedals. So I jammed my feet down on the two outside ones. Nothing happened. I was scared. What if the brakes were broke?

"I did," I yelled back at Ol' Mel.

She screamed, "Step on the middle one, Dummy."

So I slammed both feet down on the inside pedal.

And we stopped. Boy, did we stop!

Unfortunately, Ol' Mel did not. She skidded right up onto the roof of the car. Ended up upside down looking in the windshield at me.

She was NOT happy.

Sheriff J came running up. He said Mrs. Bodice was going to be fine. "But I'll have to give you a ticket. It's going to cost you $5.00."

We glumly took the ticket and drove home. Ralph sat in the back with me.

We stopped in the driveway and marched into the house. Sheriff J pulled in right behind the yellow Dodge something.

We handed the ticket to Mom, who was waiting for us on the back porch.

"What is this?" she asked.

"You see your kids got in a spot of trouble this morning with the car. I'm afraid you or they are going to have to pay $5.00," Sheriff J explained.

"What for? My goodness what happened?" Mom looked real worried.

"It's on the back on the ticket," Sheriff J answered.

"What in tarnation is D-O-V-W-A-L?"

"It's pronounced DOV WAL," I told her.

"OK, what does it mean?" Mom was getting a little impatient.

We all said it together—with the start of a major laugh coming on.

Dog Operating Vehicle without a License.

Now when Ol' Mel and I go anywhere in the 1969 yellow something, I sit in the back with Ralph.

We think she liked driving. The problem is she doesn't know she can't drive.

They Thought They Could Get Away with Anything

And now the story about the pranksters that I mentioned earlier.

Mrs. Jones teaches seventh grade. This year, she had three boys, Alex, Todd and Bradley, who loved pranks and thought they could get away with anything.

In September, they put a life-like plastic mouse in their classmate Natalie's locker. Natalie took awhile to stop screaming, but she survived the incident. The plastic mouse didn't. It was crushed.

When the three boys were questioned by Mrs. Jones, they said, "Who?" "Where?" "What?" "Us?"

They did not get caught.

In October, a boy named Leo Monday sat on a chocolate pumpkin that had been placed on his seat. His seat was in the sun. So Squish! He wore it home.

When Mrs. Jones questioned the three boys, they said, "Who?" "What?" "Where?" "Us?"

They did not get caught. They boys felt very confident.

November was prankless. One of the boys were either sick or gone all month, and Mrs. Jones breathed a sigh of relief.

In December, the cafeteria supervisor found all the spoons missing.

When the three boys were questioned by Mrs. Jones and the principal, they said, "Who?" "What?" "Where?" "Us?"

They did not get caught.

After the three boys returned from winter break, they were ready to start the hobby again. They were looking for a really good prank, maybe even one on Mrs. Jones. They started looking and thinking about how this prank might work.

Just before the end of this January, one of the boys, I think it was Todd, overheard Mrs. Jones telling the janitor that she had found plastic vomit in the hall and had thrown it into the wastepaper basket. "Ya know," Todd told his friends, "maybe we should have that vomit."

Wastebaskets are always taken to the janitor's room in the basement. The door to that room is right by the entrance where the buses line up at dismissal.

The boys decided to leave with the bus riders and sneak into the basement to find that vomit. It would make a great prank. And that's what they did.

They searched nearly the entire basement. No plastic vomit.

Finally, they found it under a large box. They tried to pull it out from under the box, but it wouldn't move. Stuck.

All three leaned against the box and pushed.

The box moved very easily—too easily. Moving the box pulled a rope that tipped a plastic bucket setting on a shelf high above the boys' heads.

Splat, squish, and three howling boys ran up the steps to the hallway and found themselves standing in front of the janitor and Mrs. Jones, who happened to be looking for the three pranksters.

The two listened to the boys' tale. Alex suspected it was a prank. But who would do it?

The janitor stratched his head, so they looked at Mrs. Jones.

Mrs. Jones smiled and said, "Who?" "What?" "Where?" "Me?"

She did not get caught.

But the boys walked home wet in the January cold. And they pranked no more.

The Wake-Up Game

You probably all have something in common with the fifth grade boy in this story since all of you are not in love with getting up in the morning. What happened to this young man changed his procrastination forever.

At about 6:50 a.m. for the last three weeks, the following exchange was heard in the Smith household.

"Bobby, are you up?' Mrs. Smith called up the stairs.

"Yeah, I'm up, Mom!" Bobby answered.

However, Bobby was not up. In fact, unless Mom had a forklift, he was not even entertaining the idea of getting up.

It had occurred to him to try. Slowly he slipped his bare foot out from under the covers. As soon as the first toe touched the cold floor, he yanked it back into the bed and resolved to stay there.

His intention to stay under the covers melted when Mom shook his bed. "Bobby Franklin Smith, get up this instant." When your mom calls you, using your middle name, you know you're in trouble.

Slowly, Bobby dragged himself out of bed and hopped across the cold floor to the rug. Unlike his sister Beth, Bobby takes two minutes to dress. Beth spends a lot of time looking at what shirt goes with what jeans. Not old Bob, he uses his nose. He sniffs the shirt. That decides what he will wear that morning. Once Bobby is dressed, he splashes a little water on his face and he is ready to meet the day—but not to meet his sister.

She'd start in on him as soon as he sits down at the breakfast table.

"Do you know you just poured orange juice into your cereal?"

"Yes, I do know it. I like it that way."

"Are you going to wear that shirt to school?" she'd continue.

Bobby was now really annoyed. "Are you going to wear that face to school?" he'd growl.

Well, the conversation went down hill from there. Bobby seldom fit fully into human form before 10 a.m.

And so the day and the game continued until Bobby's father decided to get involved.

Dad works the night shift and was trying to sleep about the time the "wake up game" got into full swing. One afternoon, Dad stopped Bobby as he came in from school.

"I think you need to stop all this waking up stuff with your mom," Dad said.

"OK," Bobby answered meekly.

Despite the warning, Bobby continued to play the game. He had forgotten how the *Garbage Game* ended just a few short weeks before.

Bobby was in charge of carrying out the garbage from the kitchen, but he had been negligent in his duty. One fine afternoon, Bobby returned home from school to find the garbage in a bag on his bed. You can imagine his disgust and anger. He flew down the stairs to deal with his sister, but he ran smack into his father. When Bobby told him what had happened, he was surprised to learn Dad knew all about the garbage on his bed.

Dad explained, "You know you are supposed to take the gargage out. Well, it piles up in the kitchen. It overflows the can and that upsets your mom. She complains. Those complaints upset me. To be honest the only one in the chain who was not upset was you."

"But what is that garbage doing in my room?" Bobby whined.

"You see Bobby, I took it out of the kitchen. That made your mom happy. She had no complaints. I was happy. Now the only one unhappy is you. I've got a hunch you will get the garbage out from now on."

Dad was right. Bobby never let the garbage overflow in the kitchen after that episode.

Before we end this adventure, we must introduce the family dog. Spike is a large, hairy animal of unknown variety. In truth, you sometimes cannot figure if Spike is coming or going. The dog's mouth can be found by waving a Milkbone Dog Biscuit near it. Spike simply loves that treat. Bobby has used those biscuits to reek havoc with his sister. Can you image what a dog and it's slober can do to a girl's purse while looking for a hidden dog biscuit?

A week or so after the purse incident, Bobby tempted Spike with a biscuit he threw into Beth's closet. After the dog dashed in, Bobby closed the door. We can say with certainty that a large dog and a small, dark closed space do not mix. Beth was in a rage for over a week.

Two weeks had passed since the closet incident when Dad talked to Bobby about the *Wake-Up Game*.

On a Tuesday morning Bobby heard a voice say, "Bobby, are you up?"

"Yeah, I'm up?" he answered. However, he was not even close.

It did strike him that the voice was not Mom's.

Bobby peeped out of the corner of his eye. He saw not Mom, but Dad and Beth standing in his bedroom door. Not a good sign.

As he watched, Beth tossed something into the air. Bobby opened his eyes and saw a dog biscuit coming straight at him. This was indeed strange. He blinked. Now he saw that right behind the biscuit was Spike, also heading right for him.

Bobby was not quick enough to escape either the bisciut hitting his bed or the impact of the dog hitting him.

There was a loud screech of springs and a thud as Bobby hit the floor. He sat there watching Spike chomp on a dog biscuit in the middle of his bed and slobber all over the covers.

If you are playing the *Wake-Up Game* and you have a dog, you are advised to hide the dog biscuits. *And* have a good escape route planned!

My Mom Is a Very Strong Person

My mom is a very strong person. She works out, works a job and puts up with my silly sisters. Me, I'm the perfect male, although every now and then I have to let the sisters know what's what. A brother has to do what a brother has to do.

It struck me out of the ordinary when Mom had to go to the doctors. I do mean doctors—at least three different ones.

Then, one evening after dinner, Dad asked us to stay at the dining room table. Mom looked tired and kind of sad. She started to tear up and blurted out, "I have cancer!" Well, none of us knew what to do.

I wanted to cry, but being a boy I couldn't. I wanted to hug her, but I was afraid I'd hurt her. I just sat there in a daze. The word cancer ran through my mind. So dumb me. I blurted out, "You're going to die, aren't you!"

Mom came over to my chair. She knelt down next to me and explained that she would be sick at times, tired at other times. But in the end, Mom said, she would be fine.

She sounded confident and she looked the same. So I decided it would be okay. Kinda. But not for long.

Mom got weak. She stopped going to work. She stopped fixing our breakfast. She stayed in the bedroom most of the day. When she did eat dinner, she just played with her food. The medicine made her sick to her stomach.

Mrs. DeLancey, a neighbor, made us breakfast and cleaned the house. We had to eat school food. No more homemade stuff.

I would run up to her room and kiss her good-bye. She seemed fine.

There were those times when she didn't know I was watching that Mom looked scared. Moms are not suppose to get scared. So I got scared, too.

I tried to help out, but Mom was not very patient. I would get mad, but I couldn't be mad at her. She was sick. So I started getting in trouble at school. I had little patience with myself or anything else.

Dad came to school when I got in a fight. He looked tired and mad. He asked what was I doing and didn't I know this was not helping my mom?

I knew it but I couldn't stop myself. I just felt guiltier about my behavior. That made it harder for me to stop.

They sent me to a counselor lady. She let me talk. Never interrupted. She said what I was doing is normal. I'm mad that my mom is sick and might die. I can't be mad at Mom, so my madness comes out in other ways.

She told me that when someone in the family gets cancer, really the whole family gets cancer. It affects every part of our life for awhile.

I realized she was right. Saying it helped. I figured I needed to get right for Mom and the family. I settled down.

The counselor lady checked on me every now and again. I was feeling a little better. I helped my sisters on occasion. A brother has to do what a brother has to do.

Then it happened. The scariest day. I came home and rushed upstairs to show Mom a math paper I'd gotten a *B* on.

I opened the door. Mom was crying! My mom was crying.

I never saw her cry like that before. It was a scared kind of cry. I shut the door quietly and went down to the kitchen.

Mrs. Delancey saw my face. I told what I saw. And I cried. I think that was the first time. Somehow it seemed odd, but okay to cry. Mrs. Delancey sat down next to me.

She asked, "Do you know what the medicine that kills the cancer does to your mom?"

Yeah, it makes her tired and sick.

"And in some cases, those medicines make you lose your hair. You mom's hair is falling out. You know how she likes her hair to look just right.

Dinner that night was very quiet.

Later, after the dishes were cleaned, dad took us out for ice cream. He told us about the hair failing out. He told us we were going to have a "Choose a wig party."

I thought he was crazy.

He brought home seven boxes of wigs. Mom tried them on. Heck, Dad tried them on. He looks terrible in long blonde hair.

We all laughed. It felt good to do that.

At the party, through tears, she told us the hair failing out shows the medicine is working. I thought if she could grin and bear it, I could, too. At least I wasn't losing my hair.

You know, it could be cool, having bald sisters. Oh never mind, forget that.

Sometimes, Mom wore a blue bandana. We called her the pirate lady—not to her face, though. She was still sensitivity about the hair.

About six months after she started the cancer medicine, she had a big doctors meeting. I couldn't concentrate at school. All I thought about was that meeting.

My sisters cried on the bus. I got them to stop before we got to the front door. A brother has to do what a brother has to do.

I opened the door, and I knew things would be all right. Dad was whistling. He only whistles when he is happy.

Dad told us to go out to the porch. Mom was out there drinking coffee. She told us to sit down.

She looked serious. But then she began to smile. "Kids the doctor looked into my body."

"It's called a *CAT scan*," Dad put in.

"What did they see, Mom?" I could hardly wait for the news.

"They saw that the cancer has stopped growing and in several places, it's shrinking."

My sisters cheered, I just stood there and cried. My mom hugged me.

"I think it's going to be okay," I said.

"Yes," she smiled.

She comes down now and has breakfast with us. She just sits there and smiles. I don't know how anyone could watch my sisters eat and smile—but Mom does.

And Mom is back to work two days a week. She has a lot more energy.

I think that counselor lady was right. The whole family got the cancer, sort of.

Mom starts back to work full time next Tuesday. If you ask me, I think it's going to be all right now.

Anyway, that's all I got to say. You see it's been a whole hour since I messed with my sisters. Gotta Go. A brother has to do what a brother has to do.

John Got This Great Idea

John watched a police movie and was impressed with the flak vests policemen wear. This is the same type of body armor that stops bullets from killing soldiers. John thought about the protection provided by the vest. Immediately he thought of another use for this type of garment.

He knew if he could invent a vest that would deflect insults and hurtful comments, he would make millions. His idea was that if a person was wearing this vest and someone said something nasty, it would bounce off the vest.

"You are a real dummy," someone would say to you. *Bong!* It would just bounce harmlessly away.

"You are ugly," would be the insult. *Whap!* That comment would hit, slide down the vest, and splash on the floor.

John was sure he had something. However, he decided his invention needed more investigation. Uncle Jim worked at the police storage facility. Perhaps John could visit and actually look at a vest. See how it was put together. Maybe even use the same type of material or design. Except, of course, the vest would have to come in some cool color, nothing like the drab olive vest worn by the police.

One Saturday morning, Uncle Jim picked up John and drove to the storage base. There were rows and rows of flak vests. John held one. He put one on.

"Boy, these are heavy. My vest will have to be lightweight. It will have to come in colors of course," said John.

"The vest has to be heavy to stop a bullet," his uncle reminded him.

"Just think, Uncle Jim, you can be shot and not feel it."

"Oh no, John, you feel it. In fact, the impact may break a bone, or at least leave an awfully painful bruise," Uncle Jim said.

"So the bullets do hurt and you don't see the bruise," thought John.

This threw John's idea in a tailspin. He was sure now his invention would not really work as well as he had planned. "Even if insults did bounce off, they would leave a bruise. You couldn't see it, but it would be there just the same?" he asked.

"Isn't that the way of all hurtful comments? You really don't see the hurt they cause," Uncle Jim commented.

"Seems to me, the best defense would be not to say something harmful to another person."

"Then you would not need a vest," continued Uncle Jim.

"So my idea is a nothing," John said hanging his head.

James Flanagan

"No, John! You brought up a great point. A point we should all remember. Insults leave marks on people, you just can't see them. That's something to think about."

"Yeh, instead of a vest, I ought invent a mouth zipper. Or at least an alarm to warn people before they say something dumb," announced John.

"You keep working, John. It's good thinking you're doing."

The Campout and the Cemetery

A few weeks ago on a Friday night, Liz, Becka, Margie and Megan decided to camp out in Megan's backyard. Now this is a typical activity for kids. It means food, fun, and gossip. But not this campout. This one was different. That is why I call this story "The Campout and the Cemetery."

Megan, also called Meg, lives in a big house right outside town. Behind the house is a large back yard and a "hollar." Beyond the hollar is a creek with a bridge over it. The bridge leads to an abandoned graveyard.

About 7 o'clock, the girls began arriving. Soon Liz, Becka and Megan had staked out their places in the old Army tent Megan's dad had set up just at the edge of the yard. The girls were just putting the finishing touches on the inside of the tent when they heard, "twenty-eight, twenty-nine, thirty."

"Margie, is that you?" Liz called.

"Yeah. Oh darn! You made me lose count," said Margie.

"What in the world are you counting?" asked Megan.

"Why, I'm counting the steps from your back door to this tent flap."

"Why?" asked the three girls.

"So I know the steps if I have to escape," Margie answered, annoyed.

"Margie, get yourself in here. You big scary cat. You are not going to need to escape tonight," Becka yelled at her.

Margie is the biggest scaredy cat in the sixth grade. They say she is afraid of her own shadow. She told Becka that she checks under her bed every night.

"No need for that here," thought Becka as she dragged Margie into the tent.

The girls settled down to eating and gossiping. Liz, who carried peanut butter to all her campouts and any other outings, started the whole thing.

"You know we ought to go out to that old graveyard beyond the hollar," she said, munching on peanut butter.

That brought Margie up to an almost standing position. "Cemetery? Cemetery? I am not going near any dead people!"

"I heard it was haunted," said Becka.

"Well, the odd thing is that the cemetery is always well-groomed. My dad cuts the grass, but somehow the weeds and crab grass never grow up," Megan explained.

"That is odd. So it is haunted," said Liz through her peanut butter.

The conversation spooked Margie so much that the girls changed the subject. About 11:30, having eaten all the chocolate in the tent, Liz brought the subject up again.

"It would be a hoot! We would be big time in school on Monday," said Margie. But then she caught herself and said, "Never mind."

"Don't worry, Margie. If a ghost got hold of you, it would throw you back within minutes," laughed Becka.

"Very funny, but haunted is haunted," said Margie.

A little after midnight, the decision was made. The fearless three plus one would track to the old cemetery. The girls gathered up their coats and flashlights and Margie and headed toward the creek. The moon was full and bright.

"It's almost like daylight," said Becka.

Right in the middle of the hollar was an old fallen tree. It was gnarled and blackened. It looked just like those trees you see in horror movies. The girls walked into its branches for a closer inspection. Margie, however, made a giant circle around the tree.

"I am not going near that old tree. It looks haunted to me," she mumbled.

The group rejoined Margie and they continued on their route to the graveyard. The moon moved behind the clouds. Megan was in the lead. She switched on her flashlight to see ground better.

This gave Liz a great idea. She walked up behind Margie. She clicked on her light and held it under her chin. It gave her a ghostly look. "Oh, Margie," she cooed.

Margie looked back, screamed, jumped, turned in mid-air and ran for the tent. It took Becka and Megan several tries to catch Margie and drag her back toward the bridge.

"Liz, give me your flashlight," Megan demanded.

"Okay, I'll be good. I won't try to berserk Margie," said Liz. "Unless she needs it," she mumbled under her breath.

"But I'm not going," said Margie.

"OK. You stay here all by yourself," answered Liz.

Margie looked at Liz and growled, "I hate you."

Margie protested every step. Despite her resistance, the girls arrived at the bridge within minutes, but once there, they began to loose their spirit.

"Maybe we need to go back," said Megan.

"No, we're here. If we don't go across, we'll be laughed at in school on Monday," Liz answered.

"Who will know?" asked Becka.

Pointing to Margie, Megan said "Guess who will tell?"

Margie just rolled her eyes.

Liz said excitedly," I got it. I'll cross the bridge and open the gate. We'll go into the cemetery. You see that big monument that looks like a pencil?"

"Yeh," the girls answered.

"Well," continued Liz, "We can all touch it and then run."

The girls agreed on Liz's plan. She slowly walked across the bridge. It creaked under her footsteps. She reached the gate and tugged at it.

"Cre-e-eak." Slowly the gate moved.

Liz pushed it to the fence and it clicked into place. She turned around to see Becka and Megan arguing with Margie. They were so intent that they didn't see Liz slip up behind them.

Liz lined herself with Margie and the gate opening and flipped on her flashlight. Sliding the light under her chin to make that same spooky face, she whispered in Margie's ear.

Margie looked up and bolted across the bridge. Before she could stop she was standing in the middle of the cemetery. "Holy Cow, what I am doing here," she screamed.

"Why you're investigating cemeteries, Margie," Liz answered.

Margie was frozen to that spot. The others walked among the tombstones looking at inscriptions. Finally, the three had seen enough. They picked up Margie and carried her to the big pencil-like tombstone.

"Okay, you guys, reach out and touch it." said Megan.

The moon had returned to brighten the scene. The big gravestone was very bright in the light. The girls began to giggle.

"See, we had nothing to be afraid of," Liz said to Margie.

At that very moment, a shadow appeared at the top of the tomb marker. It slow slid down the face of the monument.

"Run like never before!" yelled Becka.

The girls did. They ran faster than they had ever run in their lives.

Finally, at the tent, each bent over trying to catch her breath.

That's when they heard it.

"Help! It's got me! Help! I'm going to die!" came the cry out of the darkness.

"Oh my gosh, it's Margie. And something's got her!" Becka yelled.

"We've got to go get her," Liz said.

Slowly the girls, armed only with their flashlights, moved toward Margie's cries.

They had gone about ten feet when they saw Margie's predicament. That's when they started laughing. The girls walked up to the base of the fallen tree to see Margie caught by one of the limbs.

"Help! It's got me!" Margie yelled.

"Oh, cut it out. The only thing that has you is this old tree branch," laughed Liz.

"No, it's a ghost. I know it. I can feel his awful fingers," Margie wailed.

It took a little while to untangle her, mostly because the girls had to stop to hold their stomachs. Hard laughing does that to people.

Once freed, Margie ran to the tent. The others followed at a leisurely pace.

"Well Margie, do you still believe in ghosts?" asked Megan.

Before Margie could answer, the girls heard the slow creaking sound of the gate closing.

"Did you close the gate, Liz?" asked Becka.

"Noooo."

The four girls raced to the back door. They ran up the stairs into Megan's bedroom. Liz shut the door and Megan pushed a chair in front of it. They joined Becka, who peeked out the curtains in the direction of the cemetery. Margie was under the bed and refused come out. The others spent the entire night looking toward the cemetery and trying to talk Margie out from under the bed.

The following Monday, the girls told and retold their story to the entire seventh grade. While Becka, Liz, and Megan spoke of the ghostly encounter, Margie bragged about the fact that she had counted thirty-one steps from the tent to the back porch, but had make the distance in seven. "That's got to be a record," she announced proudly.

Dog Grooming

Casey is my dog. Look at her. She is a kind, loving, gentle dog with beautiful dark eyes. She is smart, but if she doesn't want to do something, she can be very headstrong.

My sister Sylvia is nine years old. I am ten. She is *always* thinking of things to get into. If you listen hard, you can even hear the wheels turning under her long brown hair.

Me? I'm her brother and I'm a joy to live with. But she gets herself and me into the darnest predicaments.

My sister decided that if we washed and cut Casey's hair, we could save Dad a lot of money. He might even decide to give us some of that extra money. Heck, we might start our own dog haircutting business. She dragged me into this and pulled me into the living room to ask Dad.

If you ask me, Dad agreed too quickly. And he had that smile on his face, like when he knows a secret. My sister didn't notice that grin.

"Are you sure of this?" I asked her.

"Oh sure, Dummy. Don't all my great ideas turn out?"

"Well, no!"

"Never mind, let's go get the hair clippers and Casey."

We found the clippers and the big tub. We put the tub on our picnic table. I filled it with warm water while Sis got Casey.

We poured water on Casey and started to suds her down. I thought this was going way too easy. I was right.

Suddenly Casey decided she didn't want to do this anymore. She flew out of that tub like a jet. We had to chase her down.

Dad just sat on the back porched and laughed at two crazed kids chasing a soapy dog around a picnic table.

When we got her back in the tub, she was dirtier than when we started. We were as wet as the dumb dog.

Casey decided to leave again, but this time I grabbed her collar. She immediately dragged me about ten feet in the dirt. Syl put Casey back in the tub. I just stood there looking like I got hit by the mud fairy.

We fought a losing battle trying to rinse her. We would spray her, she would shake. We'd hose. She'd shake. I got to figuring if someone (my sister) held the dog's head, it would stop the shaking. It did, but then as if to show us she was mad, Casey let loose a really big sneeze right in Syl's face. I had to laugh. My sister sent dirty looks at both me and Casey. Casey, by the way, seemed to be smiling. Finally we gave up and pulled her out of the tub.

It didn't take long to use up the towel that Mom gave us. Casey, the smiling dog, was still very wet.

Syl brought out the heavy guns—her hair dryer. After five minutes, Casey was still not really dry, but very puffy. We had to comb both ends to find her face. Right at that moment, I got the best idea of the day.

I asked Dad to pull out the little Honda with the sun roof. We sat on the passenger's seat and put both Casey's back feet on a box. This way almost all of her was out the sun roof. With her paws resting on the roof, she dried pretty quick.

The best part, though was watching the faces of the people we passed in the car. People stared, dropped packages, and in one case, a lady came close to hitting our car.

I told Dad we ought to do this again. He agreed. Mom didn't. Dad says she's the practical adult in the family. He said he's working on that. She did laugh when we drove to the garage. Now we were ready to cut—oops, I mean, *groom* the dog.

Casey did not like the sound of those clippers one bit. She turned and flinched and tossed her head. This caused me to chop off a little of her right sideburn. So Syl evened up the other sideburn. Then I had to even up the other sideburn. In the end, Casey didn't need those sideburns. Anyway, they're gone.

Casey moved again, I put a racing strip down her right side. Sooooo, I put one down her left side to match. It seemed only fair.

Miss Sylvia had no sense of humor about it at all. "Wait till Mom sees that!"

I was losing my patience with this grooming and my persnickety sister's comments. "Well, if you grab her legs she won't move so much."

Syl grabbed the legs. I grabbed Casey's hair, or what I thought was Casey's hair, and clipped. Syl jerked her head up and screamed. On the right side, her long brown hair was about 10 inches long. On the left, it ended at maybe 5 inches.

My sister ran for the house, Casey ran the other way. I ran for my life.

I hid behind Dad. Mom and Sylvia talked real loud and pointed fingers at me. Mom pulled Casey into the kitchen.

What we saw was shabby. Up close, it looked as if we were doing a good job. But back up and Casey was a mess. Embarassed, too. She crawled under the kitchen table and refused to come out. Mom thought she probably heard the squirrels laughing at her.

Sylvia and I got down and patted Casey. We tried to make her sad eyes go away. We said we were sorry a hundred times. At least. It seemed to make no difference. Later we sneaked her some ice cream and she forgave us.

In the end the repair—if you included fixing Casey, my's sister's hair, and my black eye (Oh yeah, I forgot to tell you that after Syl got a good look at what I cut, she punched me)—all that cost three times the money to let someone else groom Casey. So our dreams of a dog haircutting business were over before they started. After that, the incident was rarely mentioned.

Except, every now and then, Dad turns on the hair clippers and Casey runs for her life. Now I know why Dad had that grin.

Me? I've stayed out of trouble and I intend to keep it that way. Well, that is until my sister talks me into another dumb thing.

I Must Be Brave in the Attempt

Darla was a slight, brown-haired seventh-grade girl. She didn't look like a great athlete. How she became one is the rest of this story.

Darla worked hard for anything she achieved. A *B* on a math test caused celebration. Things came easily to her sister Donell, the pride of the eighth grade, but not to Darla.

As spring approached, Darla announced she would go out for the seventh grade track team. She chose her event—the mile run. Donell ran the mile in her seventh-grade year. But Darla was different. She was slooooow. She practiced hard. Every day she ran at least three-quarters of a mile. Every day her time was the same…slooooow.

Along with the mile run, Coach Corbin tested her on other events. Darla tried the shot putt, but when she hoisted it into her hand, she tipped over. Coach tried her in the discus throw. When she threw the disc, track team members all over the practice field dived for cover. Finally, he placed her only in the mile run.

The season started. Darla never bugged her coach, but every time he announced the mile runners, she stood by looking at him with her big sad eyes. He left Darla's name off the list until the next to last meet of the season. When he called off the names for that day, he paused, then named Darla. The team cheered. Darla was ecstatic. The week before the meet, she practiced extra hard and her time improved.

As the runners lined up for the mile run, Darla was so excited, she couldn't stand still. At the starting gun, the runners took off down the track with Darla in the lead.

She was still in the lead when they hit the second lap. She might score a point. At the end of the third lap, Darla was second. Surely she would score a point in the mile run. The crowd in the stands was on its feet. The team on the field cheered her on.

The runners crossed the finish line—first place, second place, third place, next runner…

"Wait a minute, where's Darla?" Coach asked.

He looked down the track. No more runners.

"There's Darla!" a scorekeeper cried as he pointed across the track.

On the far side of the track Darla was walking. She *never* walked, especially in her favorite event.

Suddenly she stopped, bent over, and threw up. Even the spectators groaned. Darla straightened up, wiped her mouth, and continued down the track. A few yards farther on, she stopped and bent over again, although this time she didn't throw up.

Some of the team members wanted to go help, but Coach told them to wait.

Darla straightened her uniform and started jogging toward the far turn. As she completed the turn, she moved a little faster.

By now, every member of both teams had stopped everything. All eyes were on Darla. As she moved toward the final turn, the crowd moved toward the finish line. Down the straightaway Darla came, moving for all she was worth. The crowd went wild.

As she crossed the finish line, she collapsed in Coach Corbin's arms. The team and the crowd closed in arounnd her. Everyone clapped and reached to pat her on the shoulders.

Isn't that strange? Why such an uproar? She didn't win. She didn't even score a point. Darla came in dead last.

But I have to tell you, when discussing that track meet, no one seems to remember who won or what the score was. But they all remember Darla and that she finished the race that day.

The Butterfly Pin

When Alice attended public school for the first time, she entered seventh grade. Up until that time she attended home school. Her family belonged to a very strict Christian church. She wore long dresses and very long hair, a fashion that made her stand out from most of her classmates. That is probably what caused her difficulty.

Alice was a good student. She was friendly and accepted by most of the students. However, one particular student named Tamara took a dislike to Alice. Tamara was a bully. She made it her business to pester Alice at every opportunity. Alice tried to ignore the situation, but that made Tamara try even harder.

One day in gym class, Tamara purposely knocked Alice down. The gym teacher saw the incident and disciplined Tamara.

Tamara swore to her friends, "I'll get even with that dorky girl. You just watch me."

One of the girls in the class told Alice what she had heard. Alice grew scared and confided in her mother. Mom listened and held her while she cried. "We must pray for an answer," she told her daughter.

The next morning, Alice's mom told her about the plan that had come to her in her sleep. "You must be strong. You must accept this trial. I will give you something to help."

She handed Alice a pin shaped like a butterfly. It was gold and light blue with shades of red in the wings and small enough to be concealed by Alice's dress collar. "This pin was your grandmother's. It will give your strength. If you are confronted by the bully, just take hold of the pin. It will remind you we love you, and it will help you to do the right thing," Mom explained.

Relieved, Alice put the pin on her jumper and covered it with the collar of her white blouse.

As soon as Alice entered the school building, Tamara jumped on her. At first, she just teased, but then she turned nasty. Alice touched her hand to her collar and kept walking toward her class. Tamara bugged her at lunch, but Alice held her temper. This enraged the bully even more.

As the students left the building for the buses, Tamara and a group of friends fell in step behind Alice. Tamara continued to taunt Alice.

Finally, completely frustrated by Alice's calmness, Tamara grabbed her and spun her around. She pushed Alice down. Alice got up and did something Tamara had noticed earlier. She touched her collar.

"What do you have there, girlie," Tamara asked in a very nasty tone.

"N-n-nothing." Alice started to cry.

"Let's see!"

She grabbed at Alice's collar and the pin fell to the ground. Before Alice could get to it, Tamara picked it up. "Look at this old thing," she laughed.

Alice tried to grab it, but Tamara was quick and turned away from her.

"I think I'll just keep this," Tamara announced to her friends.

"Give it back!" Alice choked on her tears.

Tamara had her and knew it. She threw the pin to the ground. "I'm going to crush this ugly thing." She looked around at her friends.

Alice yelled "Stop! You can't!"

Tamara pushed Alice and raised her foot. Then it happened. Alice turned Tamara toward her and delivered the best right hook of the school year.

The punch knocked Tamara off her feet and on to her fanny.

Immediately both girls began to wail—Tamara with pain, Alice with shame.

Teachers arrived to administer to the wounded. Alice was so upset she couldn't ride the bus home. Tamara was too ashamed to ride the bus.

Alice's mother picked her up and took her bedraggled daughter home. The mother had apologized to the principal for Alice's shameful behavior. The principal just smiled. The next day,

Tamara remained at home nursing a bruised jaw. Alice brought a letter of apology to the principal. She cried as she explained that she did not listen to her mother or the pin. She acted badly.

The principal listened quietly. After Alice finished, he said, "You know you may not have done such a bad thing."

He continued, "I remember a story about a cow and St. Paul. A farmer asked St. Paul if he should tie the cow up at night or trust in God. St. Paul answered, 'Trust in God and tie up your cow.' I believe God helps those who help themselves," the principal finished.

"How did the Lord help me? I needed his strength!" asked Alice.

With a big smile the principal asked, "Where do you think that right hook came from, Alice?"

Alice looked at the principal and grinned, "Our Lord works in mysterious ways."

A Promise to Eddie

Eddie was an eighth grader starting a new school. He wanted to play on the school football team more than anything he had ever wanted. When his mom registered him for school, she asked when practice started.

"Two weeks from today," answered the principal.

Two weeks later, Eddie tried out for the team. The day before the uniforms were handed out Eddie was nervous. He couldn't eat, sleep, or even pick on his sister.

When he received his pads, helmet and stuff, the hard part began. "How do I put these on?" he asked to anyone in the locker room.

Bob, one of the best players, showed Eddie where everything went on his body. Eddie was fast and volunteered to do anything, but he had real trouble remembering what he learned the day before. You see, Eddie had a secret. He hadn't told Coach or the other team members about the special education program he had been in at his old school. If anyone found out, he might not be allowed to play football.

As practice continued, Eddie excelled in one thing, running hard with the football. He was very difficult to bring down. Playing assignments were made on Friday morning. Thanks to his running ability, Eddie was going to play in the backfield.

The next week was both frustrating and glorious. Eddie loved working out with the other backs. He excelled in the tackling drills. The team cheered when he ran. However, he still had real trouble learning the fakes, the plays, and the passing routes.

The day school started, Eddie was assigned to the special education room. He refused to go to class. Instead, he went to a homeroom with everyone else. When his name did not appear on the teacher's list, she sent him to the office where he broke down and cried. The special education teacher came to the office. She and the assistant principal, who was also the football coach, persuaded Eddie to go to the special class.

At practice, the boys treated him a little differently. No one knew what to say. They really did not want to embarrass Eddie. But Eddie felt the difference. He felt stupid because of the class. That all changed as tackling drills started. Eddie ran hard and everybody cheered him on. Things were different, but not really. Eddie was still Eddie. He continued to earn their respect for his hard work.

It *was* hard to work with Eddie because he had trouble learning the plays. Bob, his friend, and two other backs taught him a particular play. It was called 23 Dive. It was nicknamed Eddie's play.

During the season, Eddie ran that play three times with no real success. However, he was so glad to be on the team, anything he could do to help was fine with him. As the games became tougher, Eddie played very little. He continued to practice every day. His teammates always noticed his efforts. He just loved being on the team.

Now the last game of the season arrived. A win in this game cinched a second place trophy. The score was tied 6—6 in the fourth quarter. "Eddie's boys," the name coach had given the team, had driven to the five-yard line. There was plenty of time on the clock. The team was going to score for sure.

Coach got ready to send in the next play. As he looked out on the field, he stopped. The quarterback was signaling for a time out.

"What does he want? "Coach asked.

Bob, the quarterback, trotted over to the sideline.

He whispered in the coach's ear, "We promised Eddie he could carry the ball one more time."

"Now?" asked the coach.

"The chance may not come again," answered Bob.

"Ok! Eddie, you're in for Robby," Coach bellowed.

Eddie just sat on the bench.

"Come on, Eddie," Bob called.

"No, this is too big. I might mess it up," Eddie protested.

The kids on the bench next to Eddie helped him up.

"Let's go, Eddie! You can do it, guy!" the players cheered.

Eddie followed Bob out to the huddle.

"Relax Eddie, It is a piece of cake!" said John, one of the linemen.

The quarterback shaped up the huddle.

"Here, we go. 23 Dive on second sound. Ready! Break!" yelled Bob.

The team moved up to the line. They dropped into their stances. Bob called the signals. The ball was centered. Bob turned to hand off to Eddie. But Eddie just stood there frozen to the field.

Finally, he started forward. As he reached for the ball, it bounced out of his hands. A fumble. The quarterback fell on it and the play ended.

"What happened?" asked the big linemen.

"Nothing. Nothing we can't fix." the quarterback answered.

No one had noticed Eddie walking back to the sideline. When they did, two players ran after him and ushered him back to the huddle.

There were tears in Eddie's eyes.

"Come on Eddie, we need your help." John the lineman said.

Coach paced the sideline with a worried look on his face. He moved a player next to him, ready to bring in the next play. The quarterback turned to the sideline and held up his hand to signal that he would call his own play.

"Ok, we are going to run 19 Keeper. Eddie you know what to do? asked Bob.

"Yeah, I fake 23 Dive."

"Make a real good fake, Eddie, Okay?"

"Ok!" answered Eddie. He stood taller in the huddle.

The team lined up. Bob called the signals. Eddie made a great fake into the line. His move allowed Bob to keep the ball and run around the left end. He was run out of bounds on the one yard line.

The team huddled. The crowd and the bench were cheering their heads off.

"This is it, guys!" Bob yelled. "Eddie, we are running 23 Dive. You are going to cross that goal line." He touched Eddie's arm.

At that moment, the team heard, "Why don't you send over the dumb kid?"

It came from the other team. Bob turned and saw the front players on defense smiling.

The big lineman John stood up in the huddle. "OK, here he comes."

The team broke the huddle with a loud roar and lined up nose to nose with the other team. Bob looked at the defense, then at Eddie, then turned and called signals. He took the ball from the center, spun and pased it to Eddie.

The lines rammed each other. For a moment, neither moved. Then an opening appeared on the right. Eddie shot through it. Two defenders hit him hard. He staggered back. Leaned forward. Broke through.

Head down, Eddie plowed across the goal line. He was so intent on crossing the goal, that he ran way past before he looked up. The other team members finally caught him at the end of the field. He ran right out the end zone. Everyone cheered and patted Eddie on the back. They danced in the end zone. They rushed back to the sidelines and the rest of the team and fans. It was five minutes before they settled down. The gamed ended 12 to 6. Eddie's boys had won the trophy.

The next year Eddie moved away. The game ball the team presented to him at the awards banquet went with him.

To this day when team members get together, the talk eventually gets around to remembering the game. Someone will say, "Do you remember the junior high game when Eddie scored?"

Everyone smiles and shakes their head. Apparently, when you do a great kindness for someone, you can replay it and get that same feeling all over again.

Don't Go

They say that a family creates its own spirit. See what you think. This particular family has a mother, a father, and a 13-year-old boy named Jason. Jason was a typical eighth grader. It should be said that he *had been* typical. Early in the fall, he changed his group of friends. His parents did not consider the new crowd "a good influence." Jason started wearing very baggy pants south of his border. He wore his dark glasses backwards when they were not in use. A few weeks later, he asked about getting an earring. His parents were not overjoyed with these changes.

Tension reigned around the house. One Friday evening, Jason and his father argued loudly about his friends. Jason stomped out of the house. Ordinarily, he walked over to his grandfather' house, but Grandpa died seven months ago, so he walked around the block and came back to the porch to sit and sulk. Later that night one of his friends called and invited him to meet at the mall Saturday morning. They were going to do some shoplifting.

"You've done it before?" the caller asked.

"Oh sure," Jason answered quickly.

"Okay, see you at 10 a.m. and be sure not to tell anyone," the caller said and hung up.

"Yeh."

Jason intended to go more out of defiance than anything else. "I'll show my dad," he thought.

At 9 a.m. Saturday morning, he started out the back door and ran smack into his mom. She handed him a box. "Here, take this up to the attic and put it in our memory trunk."

Jason was about to complain, but Mom's look said, "Don't argue with me." She returned to cleaning up in the garage.

Jason headed up to the third floor, pulled down the ladder and climbed up to the attic. It was dark and very hot. He opened a window to allow cool air and sunlight to spread through the attic. He could see the dust particles floating in the air.

Jason moved several boxes until he found an old trunk marked with his family name. It was wood and cloth and had come with an uncle to this country in the nineteenth century.

It creaked and shook as Jason pried it open. The first thing he saw was his father's army field jacket. He shook off the dust and tried it on. Big as it was, it seemed to hug him.

A whisper came out of nowhere. "Don't go."

Jason was startled. He shivered in the hot attic.

"What was that?" he muttered to himself. "Who's there?" He looked at the open window and decided it came from outside.

Jason turned back to the trunk. He found a picture of his father's high school graduation.

He looked hard at the picture and laid it aside. "Boy, does Dad look different. I wonder if he even remembers what it's like to be my age."

"Don't go." Jason was sure he'd heard it, but again, it seemed to come from nowhere.

He moved cards and letters bound together. In his search, he found his parents' wedding picture. Mom was beautiful. Dad had a big smile.

Jason thought "Hmmm, haven't seen that kind of smile in awhile."

In recent weeks, his parents had argued with him more and frowned more.

"They just don't understand," he grumbled.

"Don't go." The refrain came around. The sound seemed loud and more urgent this time. Jason literally jumped off the attic floor.

"What the heck! Who is up here?" Jason said in a loud voice. There was no answer. He turned back to the trunk.

He worked quickly, putting the box from the garage into the trunk. He moved other memories to the back of the trunk. As he started to close the lid, a picture of his grandfather fell to the floor. He used to go to Grandpa's house when he and his parents did not see eye to eye. "Gosh I miss Grandpa," Jason said aloud.

Grandpa always laughed, gave him a pop, and said, "Why Jason, your mom and dad are just parenting you."

"I don't need parenting."

"They gotta teach you the right things to do, boy!"

Jason would answer back, "They're too strict. They're harder on me than other kids' parents."

"I was just as hard on your dad. You gotta remember they are looking out for you. They're your family," Grandpa answered.

"Sometimes I don't need family!"

Jason shook off the thoughts. He stuffed the picture in the pocket of the field jacket, closed the trunk, and walked to the ladder. He had just ducked down out of the attic when he heard, "Don't go." It came from somewhere in that attic.

He stood and looked into the darkened attic. "This is one creepy attic!" he muttered.

He slid down the ladder and closed the attic door, then ran down the back stairs and slipped out the back door. He noticed his mom pushing something across the garage floor, but he kept moving toward the back gate.

His hand touched the gate. For some reason, he stopped to watch his mom through the garage window, barely aware that his hand fell to his side and the gate closed by itself.

He turned and walked toward the garage door. His mom looked up and wiped her forehead. "I see you have your dad's army jacket on."

"I'll take it off," Jason answered sullenly.

"No. Keep it. Your dad would like to see you in it. Grandpa would have, too." Mom turned back quickly to the job at hand.

A lump rose in Jason's throat.

"Hey, could you help me? I can't seem to budge this thing," Jason's mom asked.

Together they pushed the big box over to a garage wall.

"This is going to take some time. I did not realize how much time. I don't suppose you could help me out. I could use you for a couple of hours," the mother asked.

She quickly added," Oh, but you are going somewhere."

Jason looked at her and at the door for a long minute. He took off the field jacket and laid it aside. "Yeah, I'll help," he said with a half smile.

The garage cleaning took three hours to complete. Immediately afterward, Mom treated Jason to chocolate chip cookies.

The rest of the weekend passed without incident.

On Monday, Jason 's new friends missed first period history class. In second period math class, he learned that they had gone to the mall. They had shoplifted. They had been caught.

He looked at his friends' empty desks and thought how lucky he was.

Was he lucky or was it something else? I will leave that up to you.

Sometime You Have to Go with Your Feelings

Rhonda's personality matched her pleasant face. Unfortunately, her weight made her shy. If a student smiled at her, she looked down. She dieted, but the weight always returned. She felt it held her back in everything. For example, the time last year when she tried out for the Black Fork Junior High School volleyball team. Her serve was better than average. She practiced it all summer. Despite the practice, she just couldn't move fast enough and got cut. She felt even more self-conscious.

Her mother always said, "Forget the bad thoughts. Go with your good feelings."

Rhonda listened, but she never believed she could do it. She looked at herself in the mirror and remembered her volleyball experiences. Consequently, Rhonda went with the bad feelings.

Her love of volleyball helped her get up the nerve to try out for the team one more time. Her serves were even better, but she still could not move fast enough and was cut.

This time, however, the volleyball coach asked Rhonda to be the team manager. She heartily agreed. She did an excellent job and worked out in practice on occasion. She really felt very good about the whole situation even if she was not a team member.

Three weeks later, Rhonda arrived at practice to find only half the team present. Three girls had become ineligible.

As the practice closed, one team member suggested Rhonda join the team as an active player.

The coach asked her, "How about it?"

Rhonda said yes. The seven remaining girls surrounded Rhonda and clapped and patted her on the back. Rhonda received her uniform.

As she walked home, she thought, "Maybe I ought to go with the good feelings."

She ran in the back door, through the kitchen, and into her mom's sewing room yelling, "I made the team. I made the team!"

Rhonda and her mom hugged. Her mother had prayed for this day. Rhonda was so happy she sang all evening.

She worked extra hard at every practice. Her moves grew faster and smoother. And an amazing thing happened. Rhonda lost some weight.

The team was seven games into the season with a 4—3 record. The next game was against North Julian, their arch rival school in the county. Rhonda's team had never beaten North Julian in its own gym. What's more, this would be her first actual game.

Game day was both wonderful and awful. Rhonda wore her one dress to school. People nodded to her in the hall. With all this notice, she still felt shy, so she kept her head bent down.

She told herself it would turn out all right, but memories kept slipping into her mind. After school, she was so nervous she couldn't eat.

As the teams warmed up, two of the girls on the other team noticed Rhonda. They began to tease her, and the teasing took an ugly turn. "Oh look, they got a rhino on their team," one player said, and the entire team laughed.

Rhonda heard the name "Rhino." One of her teammates patted her on the shoulder. The other team members gave their opponents dirty looks.

"Pay them no never mind," Coach said.

The first game was rough, but Rhonda's team won 15—12. Rhonda got into the second game. She served her first ever time—right into the referee. The whole gym laughed. Nonetheless her defense had been fairly good. She bumped the ball to a teammate who hit it over the net. As she was subbed out, she refused to look at anyone. She felt her performance was poor. The second game went 8—15 for North Julian.

Rhonda sat on the bench keeping stats and feeling worse than the time she had been cut. "What if I get to play again?" she thought.

The third game was a close match. Finally the opposing team jumped out to a 12—9 lead. Coach called time out. As the team huddled, she pulled Rhonda into the group. "Rhonda, you're in for Judy." Rhonda bit her lower lip and looked at the floor. What if she actually lost the game for her team?

The team set on defense. They returned the ball and the rival team couldn't handle it.

Black Fork took over the serve. Rhonda rotated to server.

She looked at the coach almost in tears. She looked at her mom and dad. She saw her mom mouth "Go with the good feelings."

Rhonda served. The ball cleared the net by no more than two inches. It took the other team by surprise. She scored a point. The score was now 10—12.

"Go with the good feelings," echoed in her mind.

She served again. It went right past an opposing player and she scored a second point. —11—12.

Rhonda even smiled a little as she set to serve. She looked at the other team. Her two teasers were in the front row. Their looks said, "You can't do it."

They mouthed, "Rhino."

She heard the echo in her brain, "Go with the good feelings."

The opposing team could not return her serve. The score was tied at 12—12 and North Julian called time out. As Rhonda walked to her team huddle, she heard the words "fatty" and "Rhino." The good feelings were slipping away.

"You have to go with the good feelings, it's all you have now," she mumbled to herself.

Coach overheard and said, "You got it, girl!"

The teams took the floor again. Rhonda looked at the opposing team. One of the girls was smiling through her teeth. She silently voiced the word "Rhino."

"Go with the good feelings." The echo came again Rhonda served the ball with a hard whack. However, other team bumped it and spiked it over the net. The ball came right at Rhonda and barely hit her outstretched hands. It flew high up toward the ceiling. A teammate bumped the ball to the front line. A third girl bumped it over and North Julian could not return it.

Black Fork now led 13—12. The gym rocked with applause. Rhonda's team cheered and she rotated to server.

"Go with the good feelings," Rhonda said aloud.

She stepped back from the service line and looked at the ball. She held it up and looked at the opposing team. She stepped up to the line, smiled and served. "Here comes a Rhino serve!" she yelled.

The ball cleared the net and nicked the back line. Rhonda's team led by two points, 14—12. The crowd went wild. North Julian called another time out. Mean looks followed Rhonda as she walked to her bench. Rhonda was mobbed. The team was all over her, praising her and urging her to keep it up. Coach quieted them for her final instructions. The team broke the huddle and started back on the floor.

One of Rhonda's teammates said, "Remember Rhonda you're not alone. We're with you."

Coach stopped Rhonda and winked. "Go with those good feelings."

Rhonda stepped up, looked at the net and smiled. "Here comes Rhino serve number two," she shouted.

She served another accurate ball. It was the winning point. The team had won 15—12.

Spectators poured onto the floor.

The team huddled around the coach. Suddenly, someone noticed Rhonda still standing at the service line. A team mate asked, "Is Rhonda OK?"

"Sure, she's just feeling this moment. She's been waiting for it for a long time." Coach answered.

Rhonda finished the season and started in the final game of the year. She had learned three very important lessons.

Getting even does not work, you look the fool.
1. Keep as positive as possible.
2. And we are never alone.
3. And now you've learned them, too.

And Look at It Everyday!

Tom was a fifth grader when it all started. He and his dad watched a movie on TV. As it ended, Tom turned to his dad and said, "That is what I want to be."

"You are going to have to work every hard," answered Tom's father.

"I'll work hard," said Tom.

"You will need a booster," said Dad.

"What is that?" asked Tom.

"You need to set a goal. You must write that goal on a piece of paper…and look at it every day," Tom's father told him.

Tom immediately went to his room. He picked up an index card and wrote down his goal. Then he pinned it to his bulletin board.

Later that day, his father explained,"You will need to know what things you must complete to get to that goal on your index card."

Tom started reading up on his goal. And he looked at the card every day.

Tom failed the pull-up part of the physical education test. He knew he must pass. He worked with his father three days a week until the next testing time. Tom passed. And he had looked at the card every day.

The next year, he joined the football team. He played very little, but he stuck out the entire season. During the football season, his grades fell. He worked to bring them up. And he looked at the card everyday.

By the end of the eighth grade, he had managed to earn *B*'s in everything but math. He knew he needed to be good in math. He asked his sister to tutor him during the summer. And he looked at the goal card every day.

His high school was up and down. He played in the marching band and on the tennis team. But during those seasons, his grades fell. At the end of his junior year, the counselor told about a college that was a must to get to his goal. He would have to score well on the college tests.

He took a special course during the summer. His tests scores allowed him to get into the college of his choice. At that college, they offered a scholarship. This scholarship would go a long way toward reaching his goal. Tom would have to do well and take a high level math course before he could apply for the scholarship.

As his day ended, before he turned out his light, he looked at his index card. It was very worn by now and he had it encased in plastic.

The final day of his freshmen year in college, he learned that he was on the waiting list for an opening in the scholarship program.

He went home for the summer—and he looked at his goal every day. Looking at the card seemed to raise his spirits. He somehow felt he would get that scholarship.

Mid-summer, he learned he and another boy were the only ones left. The other student was very smart and good at math. Tom was crestfallen. His dad told Tom, "Look at the card and believe." Tom looked and believed.

Two days before the start of the college year, Tom received word about the scholarship. The other boy had won it. The other boy dropped out. Tom got the scholarship.

The rest of his college career was set toward that index card hanging on his wall. In the rough times, he would look at that card and believe.

He graduated from college and took that card with him to Florida.

The next 15 months were the roughest of his life. He worked five, sometimes six days a week. He was graded. *B* was passing. *A*'s were expected.

From Florida, he took that ragged index card to the last stop. He pinned it to his bulletin board in his room—aboard a United States Navy Aircraft Carrier. You see, Tom had reached his goal, the goal he had looked at for the last twelve years.

The three words on that card were *Navy Fighter Pilot.*

*****

So now you know about the stories. They are all over the lunchroom. Listen, you'll hear and repeat them. That, of course, is another story.

Just listen.